TWO WOOL GLOVES

by Bo Jin

illustrated by Li Li

A big snowstorm was coming, and the Squirrel family needed a warm shelter. Father Squirrel set off to find a warm and cozy tree hole for Mother Squirrel and their five babies.

He looked and looked, and finally found a hole in a tall tree.

But when he peeked inside, a deep voice grumbled,

"This is MY tree!"

It was a big black bear! Father Squirrel
frowned and went to search somewhere else.

He looked and looked, and finally found a hole
in a short tree.

But when he peeked inside,
a high voice squeaked,

"This is MY tree!"

It was a spiky little hedgehog.

Father Squirrel frowned and
went to search somewhere else.

Father Squirrel went on through the snow. He looked and looked, but he couldn't find any shelter. His feet were almost frozen.

Suddenly, he stepped on something soft.

He swept off the snow with his fluffy tail.

It was a wool glove.

"A child must have lost this glove,"
Father Squirrel thought.

"The child won't be looking for this glove in the snowstorm," Father Squirrel said to himself.
"My family can use it to stay warm."

There was just enough room in
the glove for Mother Squirrel
and the five babies.

Father Squirrel wanted to get into the glove, but it was too crowded. He had to stay outside in the cold.

The wind howled and more snow
piled on the ground. The five
baby squirrels snuggled against
their mother.

They stayed cozy and warm.

Father Squirrel curled up in front of the glove,
trying to shield himself from the cold. The snow
and wind blew harder.

Suddenly, Father Squirrel looked up and saw a boy standing in front of him. The boy was bundled up in a warm coat. But he was wearing only one glove.

Father Squirrel knew why the boy was there.

"Hey, you found my glove!" the boy said. "Thanks for taking such good care of it for me."

Father Squirrel felt terrible for having taken the boy's glove. But his family needed a place to keep warm.

As the boy bent down to fetch his glove, little faces peered out.

"Oh, I see," the boy said. "You need the glove for your family."

The little boy saw that Father Squirrel was
shivering. The snow was coming down harder.

So the boy took off his other glove and
placed it gently on the ground.

Then he smiled and turned to walk home, his hands in his pockets.

"Thank you!" Father Squirrel shouted as the boy disappeared into the storm.

"We'll never forget you!"